LILY

Seventeen-year-old Marie has had a lot to cope with in her young life. But things are getting better, especially when she gets a job working for the widower Dr Slade, looking after his four-year-old daughter, Amy.

At first, her new job seems perfect. Marie loves Amy, and Amy seems to like Marie too. Then things start to change. It seems that not everyone is happy with the new arrangement. There appears to be someone else in the house—someone who is determined to come between Amy and Marie...

LILY

A Ghost Story

Adèle Geras

SHORTLIST

First published in 2007 by
Orion Books Ltd
This Large Print edition published
2007 by BBC Audiobooks by
arrangement with
The Orion Publishing Group

ISBN 978 1 405 622103

British Library Cataloguing in Publication Data available

Printed and bound in Great Britain by
Antony Rowe Ltd., Chippenham, Wiltshire

For Sally Prue

1

I saw Zoe again last night. I was standing at the bus stop at six o'clock, on my way home from the shops. It was nearly dark and there were lights on in some of the houses. I wasn't thinking about anything much. Then I noticed a bus driving up to the stop. It wasn't my bus but as it set off again something bright caught my eye. It was her pale pink coat. She was on the bus—my little daughter, my Zoe.

I felt myself holding my breath. I couldn't help it. Zoe was there, sitting by the window, near the back of the bus. She stared right at me, with one of her hands spread out on the glass of the window. If the bus hadn't been moving, I could have put my hand on the glass too. We could almost have touched, my hand on her hand, but she was gone before I could do that.

I stood there for ages, unable to move. My bus came and went but I didn't get on. I didn't want to go home yet. I thought about Zoe. I'd actually seen her. I must have imagined it, because she wasn't there. She couldn't have been, but I knew I'd seen her. How mad was that? I'd seen Zoe again, and she wasn't even alive. She had never been alive.

My name is Marie Cotter and I want you to believe me. Every word of this story is true. This is what happened to me. I'm back home again now. Sometimes, when I think about Bowdon House, I feel as if I was someone else when I was there, taking care of Amy. I'm trying to get back to normal, but I miss Amy so much. Also, I can't stop the dreams coming at night.

*   *   *

I'm seventeen. My hair is mousy but I put blonde streaks in it. Gran thinks I look like Rachel in *Friends* but I don't really. My gran loves me. She reckons I'm pretty. She thinks nice things about me, whatever I do. She's looked after me all my life.

I've never known who my dad was. Gran says he was in and out of my mum's life all the time. Some people think that mums always love their kids, but sometimes they don't. My mum didn't like me much. I know she didn't, because she ran away and left me with my gran. My mum fell in love with a man who lived in Spain and that was that. She left me behind. I got a Christmas present from her once, but that was years and years ago. Until I was five, I used to get birthday cards.

I can't remember my mum. Sometimes I dream that she's singing to me. That's just in my head though, because Gran says she never did that. 'She was too busy going to pubs to sing to a baby,' she says. 'I'm the one who sang to you, Marie. Don't you forget it.'

Gran and I get on fine. We always have. She's not old, for one thing. She's only fifty-two and she buys her clothes in Primark and Matalan. 'There's no need for me to turn into an old lady just yet,' she says.

'That's the trouble with us in our family,' she told me once. 'We grow up too fast in some ways and not fast enough in others. For instance, we don't wait until we're grown-up before we have kids, do we? And dads don't stick around for long, either.'

She used to laugh when she said this, but not how you do when something's funny. She laughed in a way that made you think she wanted to cry, really. My mum was born when Gran was twenty, and my mum had me when she was dead young too. As for me, I was younger than either of them when I had my baby, but I was punished for that.

We live by the sea, near Eastbourne. The town is okay in the summer but dead in winter. The sea's good. It's there all the time, changing with the weather, and you can look at it whenever you're bored. The sea makes you feel small. It says, *I'll be here when you're dead. I was here before you were. I'm the sea and you're nothing, less than nothing.* I like that. I like watching it, especially in winter. The waves come crashing up on the promenade when it's stormy.

'Can it get up as far as here?' I used to ask my gran when I was a little kid.

'No,' she said. 'This estate's too far away from the front. We'll be okay. Don't you fret, pet.'

I laughed. That was our joke, that rhyme. *Don't you fret, pet.* It comforted me when she said that, whatever was wrong.

Gran works in the small

supermarket on the corner of Framly Lane. She's a manager now, but she used to be a checkout lady. I liked going to see her after school. The other checkout ladies gave me sweets. I pretended that I was helping Gran. I wasn't really. I just sat about in the canteen until she was ready to go home. Sometimes, when the boss was out, Gran let me stand near her at the checkout and I loved that. I liked seeing what people had in their trolleys. The best thing of all, though, was the babies.

Some mums don't know how to cope with a crying child. The mums I hated were the screamers. They yelled at the poor little things and made them cry even harder. Other mums tried to shut the babies up with sweeties. Didn't they care if their kids had rotten teeth? No, they only wanted a bit of peace. When she saw a baby in the queue, Gran used to wink at me. Then I went to chat to the kid. I always asked the mum to tell me what her child's name was. You can't play with a baby if you don't know what to call it. I tickled their toes. I stroked their hair. I made silly noises, and they laughed at me. Their mums sailed through the checkout with no problems.

'Isn't she good with babies?' some of them said.

'She'll be a lovely mum,' Gran agreed.

I loved the babies. I liked their silky skin. I liked their smell, of baby powder and shampoo. I liked their little fingers. I liked the way they gurgled when they laughed. I liked their tiny teeth. When they left the supermarket, I felt sad. I must have looked sad too. Gran used to say, 'Cheer up. You'll see another baby tomorrow. There's no shortage of them round here.'

I was never much good at school. I had a couple of friends, called Jeannie and Suze. They were all right. They used to come round to my gran's flat sometimes. That's on the Grange Estate, which is more grotty than rough. I never minded living there. Everyone I knew lived somewhere a bit grotty. Until I went to Bowdon House, I thought only movie stars and celebrities lived in posh mansions. I used to look at pictures in *Hello!* and *OK* but I didn't believe what I saw. I thought that I was looking at some place that wasn't real—Magazine Land.

I didn't get on with the teachers at school. They thought I was slow. I wasn't, not really, but it was a struggle to keep up. I think I was bored a lot of the time. What did I care about algebra or science? I liked history. I liked seeing pictures of olden days, but some of the books were hard. I had a problem making out some of the words. Writing was okay, but I made lots of spelling mistakes. What I think is that I didn't fall behind quite enough to get special help. I muddled along. I stared out of the window. I drew pictures on the covers of my notebooks. Jeannie and Suze helped me with homework. I got four GCSEs but my marks were rubbish. I scraped through. I was happy to leave school. I knew what I wanted to do. I wanted to be a nursery nurse. I could look after babies and get paid for it. How cool was that?

Gran was so proud of me when I was accepted for the course that I wanted to do. I felt grown-up. I went to college every day. I felt clever for the first time in my life. I was going to get a proper job in a nursery. I knew about nurseries. There was one on the Estate and I often looked in through the windows. Jeannie and Suze didn't understand.

'You should come to Brighton with us,' Jeannie said, 'and look in the shop windows there instead. There's nothing to see in a nursery.'

I didn't answer. I thought there was plenty to see—pretty dolls, bricks in bright colours, a Wendy house with a yellow roof, and lots of kids: playing, crying, or cuddling teddy-bears. A row of hooks with small coats hanging on them. I loved it. I couldn't wait to work in a place like that.

2

I met Rory at college. I was a bit nervous of the place when I first went there. I thought it was like school, but it wasn't. Lessons were called 'classes' and I liked them much better, because I was interested. I wanted to be the best nursery nurse ever. That's why I tried my hardest. The lecturers were kind to me. They helped me. There was no uniform. Then I met Rory and everything got even better.

He was gorgeous. I didn't think he'd look at me, but he did. He came to sit next to me in the college café. That was on my first day. He started talking to me. He asked me what my name was. He wanted to know where I lived. I told him, but mostly I just stared at him. His hair was dark and fell on to his forehead. His eyes were very pale blue. His eyelashes were long and thick. I wondered whether he was wearing mascara. He wasn't. I found out later that he hated make-up on lads. His mouth was lovely. I felt like kissing him, right there at the table. Later on, after we started going out together, I kissed him a lot.

The first time we kissed was at the movies. All I could think about was Rory's arm. He'd rested it on the back of the seat. He'd done that while the lights were still on. But as soon as it was dark, he pulled me towards him. Then he put his lips on mine. I'd been kissed before, but it hadn't been like this. This time, I felt fizzy inside. My mouth opened and I was warm all over. I could taste him. He touched me on the breast and I thought I was going to faint. I thought I was going to melt. I wanted him never to stop. I don't remember a thing about the movie. I heard bangs and music. I heard words being spoken. I didn't care about them. When the lights came on,

I blinked.

We went for a pizza. Rory couldn't stop talking. I was shaking. I looked at him and knew I loved him. I knew I'd do anything he asked me to do.

Everyone I know uses the word 'shag'. They talk about 'shagging' their boyfriends. I don't. I hate that word. The f-word is even worse. I loved Rory. What we did was that we made love. We did it again and again, in Gran's flat, while she was playing bingo, or in Rory's mum and dad's house when they were both at work. Whenever we were together, I was happy. Sometimes, I felt as if I was flying. I was high up and over the clouds. When it was over, I wished I could stay lying next to him, but I couldn't. There was always someone coming home in a minute.

I didn't go out with Rory for very long. It was my fault. He met Suze through me. I thought she was my friend but true friends don't do what she did. She wouldn't have flirted with him like that, not if she'd thought about me for even one second. He couldn't resist her. That was what he told me afterwards.

I said, 'What about me, Rory? What about us?'

'What about us? I still like you, Marie. You know that. I could still see you sometimes.'

I yelled at him then. 'You mean, you'd see me and Suze at the same time? Make love to both of us?'

He grinned. 'I won't tell if you don't,' he said.

I swung my hand back to hit him, but he caught my wrist. I said, 'You're a bastard, Rory. You're rubbish. And Suze is no friend of mine.'

Then I walked away from him. We were outside the chippy. I ran to the bus stop. Everyone on that bus must have seen me crying.

When I got home, Gran made me tea and said, 'You're well rid of that one, my girl.' She was right. Then she said, 'Don't fret, pet,' just as she always did, trying to make me laugh, but it didn't work that night.

I cheered up after a bit. It took a week or two, but I was getting back to being okay. Then I found out that I was pregnant. I should have felt terrible. I should have wanted to die, but I didn't. I thought, *I'll have a baby, Rory's baby. It'll be so sweet. I'll look after it and love it for ever.* I never told anyone about it at first. I wanted this secret all to myself, just for a bit.

Why do people talk about 'losing a baby'? That makes it sound as if the mum has been careless, as if she has left her kid on a bench or something—mislaid it. It wasn't like that. I had a miscarriage.

It was the worst night of my whole life. I don't want to think about it even now. There was so much blood. I didn't realise I had so much blood inside me. I didn't see how there could be any left to keep me alive.

The pain nearly tore me in half. When I screamed, Gran came running. She took one look at me and called an ambulance. I was crying so much that I can't remember what happened after that. I think the ambulance siren was on, as we drove to the hospital.

Gran sat next to me in the ambulance. 'You should have told me, pet,' she said. 'I wouldn't have shouted at you. You know me better than that. You can trust me. Don't you know that?'

I wanted to say, *Of course I trust you. I'm sorry I didn't tell you,* but I couldn't speak. When I opened my mouth, nothing but sobs came out. Gran hugged me and I cried and cried. When I stopped crying, the front of her jumper was sopping wet.

'Never mind, pet,' she said. She stroked my back and kissed my hair. 'Never mind. You'll be all right. I'll look after you.' She was crying too. 'Look at the two of us,' she smiled.

'We'll start a flood, won't we?'

Everyone in the hospital was kind to me, but they didn't know what was in my head. I thought of the child that I had lost as a baby. To me she was a girl, not just a lot of cells. I imagined her as a real person. They didn't. Well, she wasn't their child, was she? I was just another hospital case to them, even though they were really nice to me.

I called my baby Zoe. That's my favourite name. I made a picture of her in my mind. I saw her as a toddler. Her hair was very dark, like Rory's. It was wavy, too, and hung down to her shoulders. She wore a pink coat and pink shoes. Her socks were edged with lace and had flowers on them. It's not wrong to dream someone up because you're sad, is it? I told myself I wasn't crazy. I was pretending. I did it to make myself feel better.

Then, one day, I really did see her. That scared me. I was coming home on the bus from college. I'd turned into our road and there she was. She'd gone into a block of flats, a bit further down the road. I recognised her. I opened my mouth to shout but no sound came out. When I looked again, she'd gone. I never saw where she went. One minute she was there and the next minute she'd gone. I didn't tell anyone. I thought I'd made a mistake. I told myself that it was another little girl, who looked like Zoe, nothing spooky.

But she kept appearing. I saw her coming out of shops, or walking ahead of me down the street, or playing under one of the trees in the park. I saw her often. I got used to her in the end. I knew she wasn't real and I didn't mind. She was like a dream I had that came true and sometimes walked about. She wasn't a ghost—a white shape with her head tucked under her arm, or a skeleton rattling chains. I wasn't afraid of her. You can't be scared of your own child. That was who she was—my baby. The one I should have had.

I went out a lot. I walked for ages by the sea, looking at the water. I liked walking around, because there was a chance I might see her. When I came home to the flat, I did nothing. I sat in a chair and stared at the wall, or I lay on my bed and stared at the ceiling.

Gran said, 'I'm taking you to see Dr Lawson.'

I didn't want to go, but she marched me to the surgery and held my hand all the way. She knew how sad I was. I wanted to tell Gran about having seen Zoe, but I kept quiet.

Dr Lawson was a nice woman, but she couldn't really help. She said she would send me to another doctor, a mind doctor. I didn't want to go.

I said, 'I'm not mad, you know.'

'Of course you're not,' Dr Lawson said. 'But you're very low, depressed really. It's not surprising, after having a miscarriage. Dr Slade is very good with cases like yours. I'm sure you'll feel better after you've met him.'

3

Gran came with me to see Dr Slade, who worked in a hospital in Brighton. He stood up as we came into the room. He looked so kind that I stopped being scared. He was tall and had brown hair, and he wore glasses with silver rims. He came out from behind his desk and shook my hand and Gran's hand too.

'Sit down, Marie, and Mrs Cotter. I hope you didn't have too bad a journey.'

We talked about nothing for a bit. People always do that, don't they? They're working out what they think about one another. After a while, they start to speak about the real stuff. I knew this was going to happen when Dr Slade turned to me and said, 'Marie, do you like children?'

I nodded.

He went on, 'Were you looking

forward to having a baby?'

'Yes,' I said. 'I wanted it more than anything. I love babies. I was learning how to be a nursery nurse at college. I wanted . . . I knew what I was going to call my baby and everything. When I had the miscarriage—'

I stopped. I couldn't find the words to say what I felt.

'Take your time,' Dr Slade said, quietly. 'There's no hurry.'

I started crying then. I couldn't help it. I sat there and let the tears run down my cheeks. Dr Slade handed me a tissue. He never said a word. I cried a bit more and then I sniffed and dried my eyes.

'I'm okay now,' I said. 'When that happened . . . the miscarriage . . . I felt that my baby had died. A real baby.'

'That's quite natural,' Dr Slade smiled at me. 'There's nothing strange about that. You're grieving, Marie. You have to go through the grief and, in time, you'll come out the other side. I'll see you every two weeks and we'll talk things through. Meanwhile, don't feel guilty about being sad. It's okay to be sad, Marie. Don't forget that.'

*   *   *

Dr Slade was easy to talk to. I suppose that's why he was such a good doctor.

'You said you love babies, Marie. Is that right?'

'Yes. I'm studying to be a nursery nurse. I love babies.'

'Tell me about your mother.'

I didn't see why he wanted to know this. Still, it would have been rude not to answer. 'I don't remember her very well. She . . . she left when I was very small.'

'Are you angry about that? When you think of her?'

'No, not really. I think she was brave.'

'What do you mean, Marie? How is it brave? Many people would say it was cowardly, not facing up to what you've done and leaving someone else to shoulder the burden. In this case, your grandmother.'

'Gran didn't mind. She loves me. She always has. She didn't mind looking after me.'

'Do you think your mother loved you?'

'No, she didn't, but she didn't pretend to love me, either. Some mums do that. They pretend, because that's what you're meant to do. You're meant to love your kids, aren't you? But what if you don't?'

'Then maybe you shouldn't have children, if you're not going to love them. What do you think?'

Was he being stupid to test me? I said, 'She didn't choose to get pregnant. I was an accident. So was she, if it comes to that. Except that Gran loved her. Gran could have had an abortion, but she didn't.'

'Your mother could have had an abortion, too. She chose not to.'

'Yes, well, maybe she took one look at me and decided I wasn't what she wanted.' I started crying again.

'It's okay, Marie. Let's talk about something else. Tell me about college. Tell me what you like best there.'

I talked and talked to him. I told him about Rory. I told him how I hated Suze. I told him everything.

Then one day, I began to speak about seeing Zoe. Now, looking back, I'm not sure it was a good idea, but at the time it made me feel better. I just came right out with it, as if it was the most normal thing in the world. I didn't really stop to think how mad it sounded.

'I've seen my little girl,' I said.

Dr Slade leaned back in his chair. 'You've seen her? How do you mean?'

Now that I'd started, I wasn't sure how to go on. 'I'm walking down the street and there she is. She's about two years old, maybe three. She wears pink shoes and white socks. She's got dark, curly hair. Zoe, that's her name.'

'I know you want to see her very much, Marie. That's quite normal. It's also normal to imagine how your baby might have looked. But I expect you know that this little girl you saw was someone else's child? You do know that she can't—she couldn't possibly—be your baby?'

How was I meant to explain? I might be mad but I'm not totally stupid. I said, 'I *thought* she might be just another little girl. At first, when I kept seeing her. But she's . . . she's not real.'

'How do you know? What do you mean, *not real*? If you see her, she must be real, mustn't she? What makes you think she isn't?'

'She walks into walls. She came into my room at night once. When I look at her for a long time, she sort of . . . she sort of fades away.'

He looked worried. I wished then that I'd never said a word. *I bet he thinks I'm crazy now*, I told myself. I decided to make things easier for him.

'She's a ghost. Can you have a ghost of someone who wasn't there in the first place?'

'So,' he said, 'you think she's a ghost. There are people who believe in ghosts and people who don't. I don't, I'm afraid. Here's my opinion. Tell me if you don't agree that this is much more likely.'

'Okay,' I said. He was getting his words ready. Would they blow my darling little ghost away? Would I see Zoe again if he 'explained' her?

'You were very hurt, very upset by the loss of your baby. You've got a vivid imagination. As soon as you knew you were pregnant, you probably started dreaming, thinking of what your child would look like. It's very natural. Some people put together—how can I describe it—a

27

sort of Identikit in their heads. There's no harm in it. It's normal. Now with you, because of the miscarriage, that process was cut short. You knew you'd never see your child, so the dream became all you had. You built it up in your head. It became very clear, very vivid. You'd made a picture of your little girl when she was a toddler. It's probably easier to imagine a three-year-old than a tiny baby. You may even have seen a kid somewhere who fitted your dream. I can't explain the fading away, or the other things you've told me about. Still, I'm sure that what you saw—or thought you saw—was not a ghost. It was just a mixture of your imagination and a real child walking about. Maybe it was more than one child. There must be quite a lot of toddlers who look as you described. Do you see?'

I nodded. I wasn't going to argue with him. If that was what he thought, okay. I knew what I knew.

4

I went on being sad for a long time, but then I got better, bit by bit. I still saw Zoe, only not as often as before. Sometimes, days and days would go by and there was no sign of her. I wondered if that was because I'd told Dr Slade about her. I wished more than ever that I'd never said a word.

I went back to college and started spending evenings with my friends. Every two weeks, I took the bus into Brighton for a session with Dr Slade. I began to like him more and more. If I could have chosen a dad, he's what I'd have chosen. He was handsome too, like a doctor on *ER* or *Casualty*.

One day near the end of June, he said, 'I think you're much better now, Marie, aren't you?'

'Oh, yes. I'm fine. Most of the time, I'm absolutely fine. I still get upset but not as often.'

'And how about . . . what you told me a few months ago, seeing your baby?'

'I don't see her now.'

'That's good.' He smiled at me. 'I think that shows you're pretty well okay again.' He took off his glasses and rubbed his eyes. Then he coughed and said, 'Marie, how would you like a summer job? I need a person I can trust, who's good with children. I know you love children. I bet you're good with them, aren't you? I'm sure you are.'

I nodded.

He went on, 'My daughter is four. Her name is Amy. I need someone to look after her. Her mother . . . Her mother died two years ago. Her car—' He stopped.

'I'm so sorry,' I said.

I didn't know what else to say. It felt funny, to be talking about his daughter. I didn't even know he had one. I'd been coming to see him for weeks. He knew all about me and I knew nothing about him.

He went on, 'Mrs James, my housekeeper, is a little old to go running after a toddler. We're getting a nanny for Amy, but she can't start until September. I'd be happy to pay you to look after her until then. If you'd like to, that is.'

'I'll have to ask Gran,' I said. My heart was thumping in my chest. Why did he say 'we' if his wife was dead? Perhaps he just meant him and his housekeeper.

'Of course. The house is right by the sea. You'd love it. It's a bit out in the country, but you won't mind that, will you?'

'No, not a bit. I'll talk to my gran about it. Thank you,' I said.

I felt happy. I was properly happy for the first time in months and months.

*   *   *

Dr Slade's house had a name. The houses near where I lived were called things like Casa Mia, but I was going to Bowdon House. That sounded old-fashioned and posh. To get there, I had to take a bus.

Gran helped me to pack my case. She saw me off at the bus station. There were tears in her eyes when she kissed me goodbye.

'Cheer up, Gran,' I said. 'I'll be back soon. I've got a day off every week, you know. I'll come back and see you.'

'You won't want to be coming and going all the time. You'll see. Once you settle in, you won't feel like moving. You can text me though. Have you got your mobile phone safe?'

I patted my pocket. 'Thanks for that. It's great.'

Gran had given me a going-away present. It was a really good phone that took photos. The screen was swimming-pool blue and it glowed when you lifted the lid. I loved it.

'I'll send you lots of texts and phone you, too. I'll miss you, Gran.' Now I was nearly crying. She was making me feel odd. I wasn't going very far away, but she was acting as if I was off to the North Pole. 'I'll be back before you know it.'

'Of course you will. I'm being silly.'

What she didn't say was, *Six weeks can be very long if you're alone.* She would be on her own and I wouldn't.

I said, 'I'll come back and see you, Gran, I promise.'

'Right, girl. Don't you worry about me. You have a good time. You'll enjoy it there, I'm sure. It'll be a nice change for you.'

As the bus went along the narrow roads, I realised that I'd never been in the proper country before. I didn't know there was so much green in the world. Out of the window, I could see grass and trees and hedges. We passed a few farms, and drove through a couple of villages but I didn't see a single person. The sea was there too, on my right as we went along in the bus. It was sparkly, today, in the sunshine, glittering like a sheet of diamonds all spread out.

I thought, *This is too far away for Zoe. She won't come here.* I hadn't seen my kid much lately, but I hadn't forgotten her. I didn't know whether I was sad about this or not. In one way, it showed that I was getting back to normal, but all the same I wished that I could see her more often.

'This is the nearest stop to Bowdon House, miss,' the driver shouted. The bus stopped.

I pulled my case out of the rack and got off the bus. Dr Slade had written down what I had to do next. I had to phone the house when I got off the bus. Someone would then come in a car and collect me. I took my phone out and punched in the number.

'Hello? It's me, Marie Cotter. I'm

at the bus stop.'

'Hello, Marie. This is Freda James, the housekeeper. I'll let Kaye know you're there. She'll be down to fetch you. She won't be long.'

I was alone at the bus stop as I waited.

Who was Kaye? Dr Slade hadn't said anything about her. The sea lay in front of me, at the bottom of a cliff. Behind me, there were fields and, beyond them, a row of trees. Birds were singing. I'd never really listened to birds before. On the Estate, you didn't notice them. Here, they were making a lot of noise. I could have listened to music on my phone, except that I didn't feel like it. It would have sounded all wrong in this green place.

I heard the car before I saw it. Then a dark red sports car came out from behind a hedge and stopped right next to me. A woman opened the door and stepped out.

'Are you Marie? I'm Kaye, Kaye

Nolan.'

'Hello,' I said. She picked up my case and put it in the back of the car.

'Hop in,' she said.

Kaye looked like a movie star. Her clothes were amazing. She was wearing jeans and a shirt, but you could tell they cost lots of money. Her make-up was perfect. Her lips were pink and glossy and so were her nails. She had the whitest teeth I'd ever seen. Her hair was brown with ginger and blonde streaks. It looked as if she never combed it, but I'd seen styles like that in magazines. You have to be really trendy and glamorous to have hair like that, hair that looks a mess on purpose.

I didn't know what to say. She made me feel shy. Could I ask her who she was? Did she live at Bowdon House? Was she a visitor?

'God, it's good to see you. Amy's a sweetie, but she gets the better of me. I'm no good at looking after kids, I admit it. And she can tell.

Kids can always tell, can't they?'

'Yes,' I said. I thought, *She must live at Bowdon House.*

'Also, I have to work. Some people think that if you work from home, it doesn't count. But it does. It's harder than going to an office every day.'

'What sort of work do you do?' I felt silly asking her, but it was something to say.

'I help people decorate their houses. I'm a designer, I suppose. I travel a lot. But I also do a lot of work on my laptop. Thank heavens for the Internet, right?'

'Right.'

'We're nearly there,' Kaye said.

It was too late. I'd missed my chance to ask her who she was. I'd have to ask Mrs James, or maybe Kaye would tell me herself later on.

Trees grew on both sides of the long drive. Right at the end of a kind of green tunnel, I could see the house. It was the same shape as a doll's house. There were two windows on either side of the front porch, and five on the first floor. The red sloping roof, too, had windows set into it. White roses climbed up the walls. The sun was shining as we stepped out of the car.

I'd never seen such a pretty house before. How was I to know it was haunted?

5

Mrs James welcomed me to Bowdon House. She was like everyone's idea of a granny—plump, with pink cheeks and white hair in a bun. She wore round glasses in gold frames. Her dress was black and plain and so were her shoes.

First, she took me to my room. We went up the stairs to the first floor. Below us, the hall was like a square. The floor was polished wood with a big carpet in the middle of it. I'd never seen anything like it. I wanted to have a closer look but Mrs James was already halfway upstairs and I thought it would be rude not to follow her. I glanced back at the carpet and saw a pattern of flowers and leaves. There were birds and rabbits half-hidden in the greenery.

Upstairs, a long corridor stretched into the shadows.

'Your room and Amy's room are on this side of the staircase,' Mrs James told me. 'The master bedroom and guest rooms are on the other side, but I shouldn't think you'll need to go there at all. My rooms are upstairs, on the attic floor. This is the nursery, just at the top of the stairs. You've come at the right time. The house has been decorated from top to bottom over the last year. Everything looks much better now. I'll show you when you've put your case in your room.'

She stopped at a door and opened it.

'Here we are. This is your room. I hope you'll be very comfortable, dear.'

I looked around. 'Yes, thank you. It's lovely.'

It was, too, even though it was quite small. I'd never slept in a room like this before. I put my case down next to the bed, which had a puffy duvet on it. The duvet cover was white and had lace trimmings. There was lace on the pillow cases too. How was I going to fall asleep in such a posh bed?

The walls were pink. The carpet was pale grey, and the curtains had pink and grey flowers on them. They were tied back with darker pink bands. I could see out of the window and there was the sea, quite far away but still glittering. On the drive below, Kaye's car was revving up. While I watched, she drove away again down the avenue of trees. I wondered where she could be going. Then I turned to the dressing-table. This was like something in a movie, with a triple mirror. If I sat down in front of it on the pink stool, there would be lots of images of me, from every angle.

'You can unpack later, Marie. Come and see the rest of the house.'

We went off again on the guided tour. The nursery was sunny and welcoming. Toys overflowed from boxes lined up against one wall. I saw books on a shelf, and cuddly animals in a big heap in the corner. One wall had a door in it. What was on the other side? I stopped thinking about that when I noticed the rocking horse. It was standing near the chest of drawers.

'That's great!' I said. 'A rocking horse. I used to want one when I was a kid. I never had one, though.'

'That was Lily's,' said Mrs James and sighed. She looked at me and sat down suddenly on the nursery window-seat. 'I suppose Dr Slade has told you about Amy's mother?'

'Not very much,' I said. I didn't want to give away what I already knew. I hoped that if I said nothing, Mrs James would tell me a bit more.

'It's up to me, then, isn't it?' She pressed her lips together. It made her look cross. 'Well, you'll have to know. I've been working here since Lily was a baby. This house belonged to Lily's family and Dr Slade moved in after he and Lily were married. It's his now, of course, until Amy grows up.'

Mrs James said nothing for so long that I had to speak. I said, 'Dr Slade told me that Amy's mum died in a car crash.' I didn't like saying this, but out it came, before I could think of a better way to put it.

'Yes,' Mrs James said. 'It happened just over two years ago. Amy was almost two years old. We were . . . Dr Slade was— Well, it was tragic, tragic. Lily had so much to live for—a successful husband, a pretty child. The coroner said that it was an "accidental death" but there were a lot of questions . . . Never mind. I suppose the coroner knows his job. Lily adored Amy. She never left her side. It was too much, I used to say. I begged her often to let me do more for the baby. "You'll spoil her," I said, "if she thinks she can have you at her beck and call." Lily didn't care. She always laughed and said, "Well, I am at her beck and call. I don't mind. I love her more than anything." '

I thought, *I'd have been at Zoe's beck and call, too. I'd never have let anyone else look after her. I'd have done it all myself.* I said nothing, and Mrs James went on speaking.

'We thought Amy would be so upset when her mum died. Dr Slade took a month off work. He was very, very hurt, of course, broken-hearted. But Amy was as good as gold. She missed her mother, of course, but after a while she stopped asking where Lily was. I looked after her. We had nannies, too, except that young girls don't seem to want to live so far out of town. They didn't stay long, any of them. Now we've got someone older coming in September. Hopefully she won't mind being stuck out here, away from town.'

'What about—' I stopped, trying to remember Kaye's surname. Nolan, that was it. 'What about Miss

Nolan?'

'Didn't she tell you?' Mrs James frowned. 'She's Dr Slade's fiancée. They're getting married in December.'

'Does Amy like her?'

'She doesn't see too much of her, you know. Kaye is quite kind to Amy, but she's not a child-centred person, not really. And she's busy, busy, busy with her work. She won't take Lily's place as a mother. She told me once that she'd rather jump off that cliff down there than have a baby herself. That's why we really had to find a good nanny.'

She stood up and opened the nursery door. We went out into the corridor and she led me downstairs again.

The dining room had a dark blue carpet and pale yellow walls, and a long, polished table with eight chairs set round it. The lounge, which Mrs James called the drawing room, was really lovely. It must have been Kaye who had decided how everything was going to look. The sofa and armchairs in this room were huge and white, and there were scarlet rugs on the floor. I liked the kitchen best. It was exactly like the ones you see in TV adverts, so clean and shiny that you wouldn't know that real food had ever been cooked there.

'You can go round the garden later, if you like,' said Mrs James. 'I expect you're hungry. I'll get you something to eat. It will be your job to make lunch for yourself and Amy every day. Can you do that? Kaye's out now, of course, but she just has a sandwich in her study, and Dr Slade's hardly ever here during the day.'

She was putting things out on the table as she spoke—cheese, cold meat, butter, some salad stuff. Then she put a plate in front of me.

'I hope that's enough. I'll come and show you where all the cooking things are before Amy needs her tea.

I should go and see to the laundry now. Will you be all right on your own?'

'Thanks, that's fine, only . . .'

Mrs James put her head on one side. 'Yes?'

'I just wanted to ask, where's Amy? Is she asleep?'

'Oh, I'm so sorry, I should have said. Amy does go out from time to time. There's a playgroup every Monday and Wednesday morning, and on Thursday she plays with Maisie. Maisie's mum is a friend of Kaye's. Kaye takes Amy there in the morning, and the little girls play together. That's where Kaye has gone. She drives over again at lunchtime to have a meal with Maisie and her mum, and then she brings Amy home. They'll be back at about three o'clock. I'll see you later. Do look round on your own when you've finished eating.'

Mrs James left the room. I sat staring down at my plate. I wasn't hungry. There was so much to think about. Mainly, though, I wanted to see Amy. What would she be like? Most of all, would she like me?

6

I went back upstairs after lunch. The house was very quiet. I unpacked my case. My clothes didn't take up much space in the chest of drawers. I had only a couple of things to hang up in the cupboard.

I sat on the pink dressing-table stool and took the phone out of my handbag. Maybe I could take a picture and send it to Gran. She'd have a fit if she could see where I was staying. I opened the silver lid and waited for the screen to light up, but it didn't. There was no signal.

How could there be no signal here? What could I do? I would have to ask Dr Slade whether I could phone Gran on a landline. Maybe if I went to the window I'd get a signal. Yes, there was the swimming-pool colour. I punched in Gran's number, feeling happy for a bit. It didn't last long. The signal went away again. I tried sending a text, but the screen showed 'message not sent' over and over. I'd have to try later.

I felt sad, all of a sudden, and lonely. I was far away from Gran and everything I knew. *That's mad*, I told myself. *You're only forty minutes away by bus. That's not far. There's nothing to be sad about. This is a great house. Mrs James is nice. Dr Slade is lovely. Kaye's okay.* That made me smile. *Kaye okay* was quite funny, for me.

It was now half past one. Amy would be home soon. I put my phone into my jeans pocket and went out to the landing.

I looked towards the high white door of the master bedroom at the end of the corridor. Mrs James had said I could explore. She didn't mean the bedrooms, I was sure. Still, she wasn't around. No one would find out. I went to the white door and opened it.

The bedroom was done up in

shades of beige and coffee-brown and gold. It was beautiful. I could see Kaye's perfume bottles on the dressing-table. There was a painting over the bed. It was a view of a garden, full of summer flowers. There was a stack of thick books on one of the bedside tables. *Dr Slade must sleep on that side*, I thought. His books were piled into a tower that looked a bit wobbly. On the bedside table on Kaye's side, there was a book called *Light on Snow* by Anita Shreve and a tube of handcream. I left the room quickly, making sure to close the door behind me.

As I came to the top of the stairs, I saw a door that I hadn't noticed before. It was next to the nursery. How had I missed it? I opened it, and went into the room. The walls were very pale lilac. There was a single bed against the right-hand wall, covered by a shabby old quilt. You could tell it was very old because the colours were faded. I wondered why this room hadn't been painted. It really needed it. I could see dark patches on the ceiling, and in the corners. A small desk and chair stood against the wall opposite the door.

On the left-hand wall, there was another door. *This room*, I thought, *is what's behind that door in the nursery*. I tried to open it, but it was locked. It felt chilly in here, even though it was quite warm outside. I worked out that it must be because no sunshine was coming in. The room didn't have a window. Rooms without windows are a bit odd. You feel as if you're in a prison. The light is strange, too.

Just then, my phone rang. I took it out quickly. Maybe Gran was trying to reach me. I flipped open the lid. The screen was doing odd things. Whitish streaks were moving about on the swimming-pool blue. It looked like one of those marbles with swirly insides. 'You have one new message' flashed on to the screen and was gone.

I went to my messages. There it was again. The screen said that I had 'one new message'. I clicked the buttons to open the text and the screen went black. I closed the phone and opened it again. No blue screen, no signal, nothing at all. Just a small black square. The room was colder than ever. I went out on to the landing, closing the door behind me.

*   *   *

I loved Amy from the very first time I saw her. You always know, when you meet someone for the first time, if you're going to like them or not. Sometimes—it happened to me when I met Rory—you fall in love with them. I think there's a kind of 'love at first sight' that you can get with kids, too, and that's what happened with Amy.

She came running towards me

53

across the flowery carpet. I said, 'Hello, I'm Marie.'

She wasn't a bit shy. She smiled at me straight away and said, 'Are you my nanny?'

'For a little while, yes,' I said.

She was very pretty. She had short, brown hair cut in a fringe. Her eyes were round and dark, with very long lashes. Her pink jeans and T-shirt matched her trainers. She had a pink bag in her hand and was holding it tight.

'I've got toys,' she said. 'Come and see.'

She gave me her hand and that was that. I loved her.

I felt happy and sad at the same time. I wished I could stay in this perfect house for ever, just looking after Amy. I wished I didn't have to leave in six weeks and go back to the Estate. Part of me was trying to work out whether there was any way that I could stay on. Maybe I should ask Dr Slade if I could. No, that was stupid.

He'd already hired a proper nanny—an older woman. He probably wanted someone who could teach Amy too, a teacher as well as a nanny. I couldn't teach Amy.

I felt guilty thinking this. What about Gran? She'd be upset if I never went home. *Pull yourself together*, I told myself. *Enjoy the time here while you can.*

In the nursery, Amy showed me her toys. She had everything: bricks and dolls and paints and paper and books. She had a pram to push her bigger dolls in. A doll's house had a set of smaller dolls living in it. She had puzzles and Lego and Play-doh. There were more toys in this room than in some of the nurseries and play schools I'd visited. There was also the rocking horse.

'He's lovely,' I said. I pushed him gently and he started to rock.

'I can't ride on him,' Amy said. 'He's old. I'm too big.'

'Did you ride on him when you

were smaller?'

Amy thought about this. 'Yes,' she said at last. 'My mummy held me on.'

I changed the subject. 'Let's do a jigsaw,' I said, moving over to the table. 'I love jigsaws.'

We sat there for ages, fitting together a picture of the seafront at Balamory. That's the cartoon town on *CBeebies*. All the time that we were working on the puzzle, Amy never let go of her bag. I said, 'Why don't you put your bag down, Amy? Then you can use both hands for finding bits of Balamory.'

Amy hung on to it even tighter. She wasn't going to let go.

'It's okay,' I said. 'You hang on to it if you want to. I won't take it away from you.'

She smiled at me. 'My phone is in it,' she said. 'I can show you.'

'Go on then,' I said.

She unzipped the bag and took out a small, silver mobile. It wasn't a toy. I wondered who'd given it to Amy. I opened it up and the screen was black. It wasn't working. Maybe it needed recharging.

'It's my mummy's phone,' Amy said, taking it from me. 'I can hear my mummy. Listen. Can you hear her?'

I had to make a real effort not to cry. Poor little thing! It was so sad that she was pretending to speak to her dead mum. Did her father know she did that? Did he even know that she had her mother's phone? He might have given it to her. Should I ask him about it?

Amy was holding the phone out to me, so I took it. I pretended to listen at first but then I heard something and I nearly jumped out of my skin.

'Is she there?' Amy said. 'Can you hear her?'

'No, no, I didn't hear her, Amy. Never mind. Let's get on with the jigsaw. Put the phone away now, pet. Okay?'

She nodded and put the phone

back into the pink bag. Then she smiled at me.

'I like Balamory. It's in one of my favourite TV shows.'

I'd taught her how to find the corner pieces of the jigsaw, and the straight bits at the top and bottom. She looked very hard at each piece and thought for ages before she tried to fit them together.

I helped her but I wasn't thinking about the jigsaw. I was remembering what I'd heard on the phone, a moment ago. Perhaps I'd imagined it. It wasn't a voice. It was a bit like the sound you hear when you hold a shell up to your ear. Gran says that it's your own blood rushing round your head and it just sounds like the sea. This was probably the same thing. It wasn't . . . *it couldn't be* . . . Lily. That was crazy. I knew that. It must have been something—well, just something I knew nothing about.

'You're very clever,' I said. 'You're good at finding how the bits of jigsaw fit together.'

'Are you staying for my tea?' Amy asked.

'Yes, I'm going to have tea with you, today and every day. Then I will give you a bath and read you a story before you go to sleep.'

'Yes.'

The puzzle was finished. We'd put together the pink, blue and yellow doors of the Balamory houses. The sea was there. So was the sky. Mothers never died in car crashes in Balamory.

7

I liked looking after Amy. It wasn't boring but it was tiring. When you're in charge of a kid, you don't get any time to yourself. As soon as you open your eyes in the morning, it's non-stop.

Amy always woke up early. On my first morning at Bowdon House, she came running into my room and jumped on the bed.

'Get up, Marie. It's day now!'

So I got up and went to the bathroom, and washed and dressed as quickly as I could.

While I was in the shower, Amy waited in my room, sitting on the dressing-table stool. She was looking at lots of different Amys in the triple mirror when I came back.

'Who's in the mirror, good Amys or naughty Amys?' I asked her.

'Good Amys!' she said, as if the

idea of a naughty Amy was silly. 'And Mummy was there,' she said, pointing into the glass. 'In that bit.'

I thought, *I must ask Dr Slade what to say when she talks about her mother.*

While I played with Amy in the garden, I thought of what I'd tell him. I didn't want to mention ghosts because of what I'd told him about Zoe. I didn't want him to think I was being mad again. I'd told him I was fine. I *was* fine. I hadn't seen anything strange for ages.

After a while Amy and I went into the Wendy house. This was a red plastic cube with a yellow roof, and gaps where the windows were meant to be. It was on the grass, just near the kitchen door in the garden at the back of the house.

The garden was huge. Mrs James told me that it went as far as the big group of trees a long way off. After that, the land belonged to someone else. That still seemed a lot of garden to me. It was mostly lawn, with a few flowerbeds cut into it. At the front, there was the long drive down to the main road. It looked like a small park, and not like any garden I'd been in before.

I was still thinking about what to say to Dr Slade. I wondered whether I should tell Gran about what had happened. I found out soon enough that my phone worked okay outdoors.

'I don't know why it doesn't work in the house,' I told Gran when I rang her.

I kept an eye on Amy the whole time that I was talking to Gran. She was busy putting out pink and blue cups and tiny saucers.

I went on, 'But it doesn't matter. The garden's lovely here. We're having a dolls' tea-party. Well, Amy is and I'm talking to you. I can phone you lots and text you. I can read your texts too. Don't worry if you don't hear from me. It just means that I'm busy. It's hard work, isn't it, looking after a small kid?'

'You've said it,' Gran laughed. 'Now you see what I had to go through. Twice. Once with your mum and once with you.'

'I've got to go, Gran,' I said. 'Amy wants me to join in. I'm going to come into Eastbourne and see you next Thursday. Okay? Great. Bye.'

Maybe I'd ask Gran about the strange things I'd heard on Amy's phone. Meanwhile, I could tell Dr Slade about them when he got home.

*   *   *

I was helping Amy to put on her pyjamas when her dad came into her room to kiss her goodnight.

'Hello, little one!' he said, and picked her up and hugged her tight. She giggled and kissed him on the cheek. 'I'm sorry I'm so late.'

'Daddy! Have you come to play?'

'Not tonight, chicken. It's nearly

your bedtime. I'll read you a story though. How about *Blue Kangaroo*?'

I got Amy settled in her bed and then Dr Slade stretched out on the duvet next to her and started to read. I didn't know whether I was meant to stay. I picked up Amy's towel and left the room.

'Marie!' Amy called out. 'Come and hear the story.'

'I'm putting your towel back in the bathroom. I'll be there in a minute.'

I took a long time on purpose. I waited outside Amy's room until the story was almost over. Then I went in. Dr Slade was about to go down to have supper with Kaye so I wasn't going to be able to talk to him tonight. I wanted to get him on his own.

'Goodnight, Amy,' he said, kissing her on the head.

'Goodnight, Daddy.' He went out of the door and I heard him go downstairs. I was on my own with Amy.

She wriggled down in the bed.

Then she turned over on to her front and pulled the duvet up so far that I could only see the top of her head.

'It's time to go to sleep, Amy,' I said.

I didn't really know what to do. I'd never tucked anyone up in bed before. I bent over her and tried to smooth down the duvet. She sat up at once and pushed my hand away.

'Nononono,' she said. 'No! Mummy tucks me in. Not Marie. Mummy!'

She was wailing. I was scared. What if they heard her downstairs and came up to see what was wrong? Dr Slade wouldn't think much of me as a nanny. He'd think I was useless.

I said, 'Okay, Amy. Don't worry, I'm going. I'll go, okay? Will you go to sleep if I go?'

'Yes,' she whispered.

I switched off the bedside lamp. It was dark in Amy's room. The curtains were thick and you'd never have known that it was still sunny outside. I left the door half open. I waited outside for a bit, to make sure Amy settled down. Then I heard her speak.

'Goodnight, Mummy,' she said. She said it quite clearly. There was a pause. Then she said, 'Don't let the bugs bite!'

I shivered. Gran and I did that. Gran always said, 'Goodnight, sleep tight,' and then I had to say, 'Don't let the bugs bite.' Poor little Amy was still pretending that her mum was saying the first bit of the rhyme.

I walked along the corridor and the door of the room next to the nursery was open. I was almost sure it had been closed when Amy and I were on our way back from the bathroom. I put my hand out towards the doorknob, ready to close the door, but a draught blew it shut before I could reach it. *Someone must have left the garden door open*, I thought. But it hadn't been windy earlier in the day. I told myself that perhaps the weather was changing.

8

Over the next few days, I saw that getting Dr Slade on his own was going to be a problem. He came home too late most evenings. I was going to have to wait until the weekend. We were going on a picnic at the beach on Saturday. Maybe I'd have a chance then.

I was looking forward to the picnic almost as much as Amy was. We spent ages on Friday deciding what toys to take. Amy kept changing her mind about who was going with her. First, Mr Snuggly, her best bear, was the one she wanted, but then she decided on Ruby, her baby doll. Once she'd worked that out, we had to pack all Ruby's things—her changing-mat, her bottle, her pretend nappies. I tried to persuade her that Lulu, the more grown-up doll, would enjoy a picnic more, but she wouldn't have it. Ruby was coming and that was that.

I put her to bed early the night before. We'd been out in the garden all afternoon and she was tired by half past six. I'd learned not to tuck her in. It still made me feel funny, to hear her speaking to someone who wasn't there, but I told myself there was no harm in it. I always listened outside the door, to make sure Amy was okay.

'Marie?' She was calling me. What could have happened?

'I'm here, Amy. What's the matter?'

'I want you to kiss me goodnight, too.'

'Yes, of course.'

I bent down and kissed her on the cheek. Then I left the room. On my way downstairs, I thought about what she'd said: 'I want you to kiss me goodnight, too.' She thought someone else, apart from me, was kissing her goodnight. Did she think it was Lily?

I had to tell Dr Slade what was going on. Perhaps he'd talk to Amy and make her ghost vanish, just as he'd persuaded my Zoe to go away.

*   *   *

Later on that evening, I went as usual to Mrs James's sitting room. She liked a good gossip. That was lucky for me. I think she must have been a bit lonely, too. On my first day, she'd told me that I could come in and watch television with her if I felt like it. That was kind of her. Her rooms were on the attic floor. The first time I went in there, I worked out that her windows were the ones set into the roof.

The only photos of Lily were in Mrs James's room. She was very proud of them. The very first time I visited her, she picked up one of the framed pictures and handed it to me.

'Wasn't she a beauty? This is her

wedding photo.'

'Yes,' I said.

Lily was just like her name. She was as tall as Dr Slade. Her wedding dress had a high neck and long sleeves. It looked as if someone had poured white satin all over her body. She was very thin and she had long, blonde hair. She was smiling. She looked so happy. It was hard to imagine her lying in a coffin. I shivered.

'Lovely,' I said, handing the frame back to Mrs James.

I got into the habit of watching TV with her after supper. She made us cups of milky coffee to drink. She did her knitting all the time, whether we were watching TV or just chatting.

That evening, she was in her room as usual.

'Hello, dear,' she said. 'Come in. *EastEnders* is going to start quite soon.'

'Thanks.' I sat down in the armchair opposite the TV.

70

'You're getting on very well with Amy, aren't you? I'm so pleased. It's nice to see her happy.'

'She's so sweet. I'll miss her when I have to go.'

'Well, let's not think about that. That's some weeks away yet. Since you came . . .' Mrs James paused in her knitting.

I could feel that there were things that she was longing to tell me.

She went on, 'It hasn't been easy, Marie, none of it. My darling Lily . . . Well, the coroner said it was an accidental death, but Lily would never drive too fast and she would certainly never drink and drive. Still, that is what the coroner said, that she was over the limit for alcohol and driving recklessly. No one but me seems to think there's anything funny about that. But do you want to know what I think? I've not told Dr Slade because—well, what good would it have done? I think Lily found out that he and Kaye . . . I can't prove it, but I reckon Lily knew something was going on between them. Kaye was her best friend, which made things worse. It's my belief that Lily—'

'Lily what?'

'Lily meant to drive her car into that tree. She meant to die. I haven't said a word, of course. It's best to keep quiet about things like that.'

What could I say? Mrs James was still talking.

She said, 'It wasn't more than a couple of months after the accident that Kaye moved in here. There was trouble with Amy as soon as she did.'

'Amy doesn't like Kaye very much, does she?' I said. 'I've noticed that. She never asks her for anything.'

'Well, Kaye's not interested in her, not really, however much she tries to pretend for Dr Jack's sake. Amy can see that she's not interested. I remember the first time that Kaye tried to put Amy to bed . . . I'll never forget that night.'

Mrs James was well into her story by now. She'd even put her knitting down on a table by her chair.

'One night, soon after she moved in here, Kaye was putting Amy to bed. Everything was perfectly normal. She'd given the child a bath, watched her brush her teeth and then she took her to her room. But when she came to cover Amy up with her blanket, the poor little mite began to scream and cry. I heard her from up here and I came running downstairs to see what was wrong. I found her completely uncovered and beating her fists on the mattress. Her little legs were thrashing about. Kaye was standing in the corridor outside, shaking. Amy was beside herself. I'd never seen her like that, never. She's an even-tempered child, isn't she? You've been with her so you know what she's like. Anyway, I picked her up out of the cot and cuddled her, sitting on the chair that stands by the window. Lily used to sit in it to feed her, when she was still breastfeeding. "Mummy!" Amy sobbed. "Mummy tucks. Mummy tucks." Well, I can tell you, Marie, it gives me a shiver up my back just to remember that night. I can still hear those words and how sad she sounded as she said them.'

'What did you do?'

'I said, "Why can't Kaye tuck you in, Amy? She loves you." But Amy was having none of that. She clung to me and I knew that she didn't want Kaye to tuck her in. She'd worked out, as young as she was, that her daddy's new lady wasn't as good as her mum.'

Mrs James picked up her knitting again and the only sound in the room was the click of her needles. Should I tell her that Amy's mum was still tucking her in?

'I bet she was jealous of her dad liking someone else,' I said. 'Kids know about things like that, don't they?'

'They do indeed. And it's Dr

Jack's job to understand jealousy and suchlike, isn't it? He started hiring nannies to help look after Amy. He knew it was no good asking Kaye to do anything for her.'

'But they didn't stay long?' I said.

'No. One said she felt lonely so far from the town. Another told me that Amy didn't really like her. Then there was Bridget, who said . . . Well, I had high hopes of her but she said . . .'

'What? What did Bridget say?'

'She said Lily came to her in her dreams. She was scared.'

I sat in silence for a moment. 'Do you think Amy's just pretending to see her mum? Really?'

'Of course she is! Lily has become like an imaginary friend. Lots of children have imaginary friends. I don't think there's any harm in it. Is it nearly eight o'clock? We'd better put the TV on, then. We don't want to miss *EastEnders*.'

She turned to the TV and I didn't

feel I could ask her about anything else. Did she know who had given Amy a real phone? Had that phone once belonged to Lily?

I'd made up my mind to speak to Dr Slade, so I decided to ask him about that as well.

9

The picnic on the beach was great. I was having such a good time that I almost forgot that I was going to ask Dr Slade about Amy's phone until quite late.

We ate and ate. The picnic food wasn't just sandwiches. Mrs James had cooked chicken drumsticks and buttered bread rolls. There were plastic bowls of salad and fruit salad, and a big tin full of fairy cakes with pink, blue and white icing. We had fruit juice to drink and that was cold, too. The whole picnic was packed into one of those bags that keeps food chilled.

After lunch, we played games and went down the beach looking for pretty shells. Amy picked up a few and put them into her handbag. *They'll scratch the phone*, I thought. *Should I tell her?* Then I thought, *It's not a real phone. It doesn't really matter if it's a bit scratched. Amy's happy. That's the main thing.*

I got my chance to talk to Dr Slade at last. Kaye had gone back to where the rugs were laid out. She was lying in the sun, with sunscreen on her face and arms and legs. Amy was busy down by the rock pools. She was talking to things under the water. She wouldn't hear what we were saying unless we started shouting. It was just him and me.

'Dr Slade, can I ask you something?'

'I wish you'd call me Jack,' he said. 'You're not a patient any more. You're like one of the family.'

I nodded but knew I'd never be able to call him Jack. That meant I couldn't call him anything. And I didn't feel like a member of the family. I don't know what I was, but a member of the family wasn't it.

I said, 'It's about Amy. Have you seen her phone? The mobile that she carries in her bag?'

He sighed and sat down. I sat down next to him, because I didn't know what else to do. He began to draw a pattern on the sand with a sharp stone. He didn't look at me as he spoke.

'Yes. I . . . I gave it to her. I thought . . . It was Lily's phone. I couldn't bear to throw it away. Lily used it all the time. She and Amy had a game they played with it. Lily was teaching Amy the alphabet using text messages, something like that. I thought later that it would ease Amy's pain a little. It seems to have worked, too, doesn't it? She loves that phone. I don't see anything wrong with her playing with it. You're not worried about the health aspect, are you? It's not charged up. I'm against young children using charged mobile phones.'

'No, that's not what I meant. She . . . Amy talks to her mum on that phone.'

I couldn't say, *And her mum talks back to her*, because that was only what Amy had told me. She was four years old and good at pretend games. She heard her teddies and her dolls talking, too, didn't she?

'That's quite normal, Marie. Don't worry about it, honestly. It's a way of dealing with grief. You know, better than most, that grief can make us imagine all kinds of things. She's good with you, isn't she? I reckon that if a child is eating well and sleeping well and is happy during the day, then there's nothing to worry about.'

'Okay,' I said.

I didn't dare to tell him about the things that *I'd* heard and seen. The funny swirls on the phone. The open door of the little room. My own phone not working in the house. To be fair, I didn't know that the lack of a signal was anything to do with Lily, but it might have been.

'As long as you're around,' he said,

'I'm quite sure no harm will come to Amy.'

That made me feel so happy that I forgot my worries. It was easy not to think about Lily out in the warm sunshine. I forgot about her and went to help Amy. She wanted to find a fish, but a small crab was the best thing I could find to show her.

*　　　*　　　*

I met Gran in town on the Thursday after the picnic. I chose Thursday for my day off because that was when Amy went to play at her friend Maisie's house. After Kaye had dropped Amy off in the car, she and I went on to Eastbourne together. She had some work to do there.

'I'll see you back here at three o'clock, Marie,' she said, before she zoomed off. 'It works out quite well, this plan, doesn't it? We can do it next week too, if you like.'

'Yes, thanks very much. That's great.'

Gran met me in the town centre. The streets seemed too busy and too crowded. It was funny that I thought that, after such a short time in the country. I'd been brought up in Eastbourne, but the noise of the traffic that day got on my nerves. Everyone seemed to be talking too loudly on their mobile phones.

Gran and I were going to have lunch in a café. Before that, though, we did a bit of window shopping. I wanted to get something nice for Amy.

'It's hard,' I said. 'She's got so many toys.'

'I don't know why you're bothering, then,' said Gran. 'It seems to me that you're the only one giving that child proper care.'

I'd told Gran about life at Bowdon House. I'd told her almost everything.

'I know, but I want her to have something she can play with when I'm gone. Something to remind her of me.'

In the end, I bought a little pink velvet pig. It was so pretty that I couldn't resist it. It would fit in her handbag. I'd say it was called Poppy.

At lunch, I told Gran about Lily, and what Amy had said about her mother tucking her in. I hadn't meant to, but I did in the end. I wanted someone to say, 'No, you're not mad.' But Gran didn't believe in ghosts.

'It stands to reason. She's pretending that her mum's tucking her in. It comforts her. You used to call for your mum to do the same thing, after she left you for me to look after.'

'I know, but it's not the same. All kids cry for their mums. Amy doesn't. Amy knows her mum is tucking her in.'

'She can't, pet, can she? Her mum's dead.'

I sighed. 'I know. That's what I'm saying. I think there's a ghost in the house—'

'Rubbish! It's just the games of a kid, pretending.'

I didn't say anything. I couldn't think of an answer.

Gran went on, 'And of course she's talking to her mum on the phone. You used to do that, too.'

'What?'

'You used to talk to your mum on the phone. We didn't have mobiles but you often used to pick up the real phone. You chatted into it for ages. When I asked you who was on the other end, it was always Mummy. I gave up asking after a bit.'

I tried to remember, but I couldn't. Maybe Gran was right. Maybe what Amy was doing was normal.

I said, 'But what about me? What about the text message that never got to me on my phone? And the swirly noise I heard on Amy's mobile?'

'All sorts of things can happen with mobile phones. You can't tell where you are with mobiles, most of the time. And you've got such an imagination, Marie. You know you have.'

I couldn't deny it. I hoped Gran was right.

She changed the subject then. She was much more interested in whether I thought Lily had killed herself.

'How do I know, Gran? Mrs James says Kaye was Lily's friend. Dr Slade was having an affair with her and Lily found out. That's meant to be why she killed herself.'

'If she was such a good mum, though . . .' Gran began.

'What difference does that make?'

'She'd never have killed herself. She wouldn't have left Amy alone. Well, would she?'

I thought about that.

'Okay, that's true,' I said. 'But what if she went a bit mad when she heard about the affair? Let's say she drank too much. Then she went out

85

in the car, for some other reason, but by then she was drunk. So she wasn't quick enough in her reactions to stop the crash. Maybe it was something like that. So it could have been half her fault and half not her fault, if you see what I mean.'

'It could be,' Gran said. 'Yes, that could be how it was, I suppose. Anyway, we'd better get moving. You don't want to keep Miss Nolan waiting. I'm glad I'll be getting a look at her!'

On our way down to where Kaye was going to meet me, I kept on thinking.

I said, 'Gran, what if Lily felt guilty?'

'Are you on about Amy's mum again?'

'Yes. What if she felt guilty? What if her spirit can't rest because of the guilt? What if she comes back to look after her little girl because she feels so bad about leaving her?'

'Blimey, Marie, you've got it all

worked out, haven't you? Well, okay, if I thought ghosts did exist, that would be a good reason for a mum to come back to earth, to look after her kid. But I've never heard of it, not ever. Have you?'

'No. But that doesn't mean it couldn't happen.'

'If you believe all that nonsense, I suppose anything *could* happen.'

Kaye was waiting by the car when we got there. She was chatty and smiling, and Gran was thrilled to meet her. I knew she'd already forgotten about Lily. I could see that she had, from the way that she and Kaye were laughing together like old friends.

'Bye!' Kaye called merrily out of the window as we drove away. To me she said, 'Your gran's lovely, isn't she?'

'Yes, she is,' I said.

I didn't want to worry about Lily any more, so I thought about Poppy Pig and hoped that Amy would love her.

10

I had my first bad dream that night.

I was in a corridor. It wasn't the corridor in Bowdon House, nor the one in the hospital. It was just a long, dark place and in it a wind was blowing. I didn't feel cold in the dream, but tears were coming out of my eyes. They didn't come one by one, like in normal crying, but in a kind of stream. The water poured down my cheeks and I was walking in it at the same time, walking in puddles made by my tears. Someone was talking. I couldn't hear what they said, however hard I tried. The voice was a murmur, and not being able to hear the words was like a kind of itch that I couldn't scratch. It annoyed me. I kept on striding through the puddles, crying, listening, being irritated that I couldn't hear properly.

Then a door slammed somewhere and there was nothing all round me but darkness. I felt as if I was down a well, or locked in a cupboard, or shut in a box. There was nothing but blackness all round me. Then I heard words in my ear. It was just as if someone had come up behind me. *Don't you dare*, said the voice. *Don't you dare to think you can. Don't. Don't you go near her. Don't you dare.*

I made myself wake up. You can sometimes. I lay in bed with my eyes closed, still half in the dream. I'd been thinking too much about Lily, that was clear. Gran would tell me to pull myself together. I got up and sat down at the dressing-table. It was nearly morning.

I don't know what made me look at my phone. It was just there on the dressing-table, where I'd left it when I went to bed. Even though I knew it didn't work indoors, I picked it up. The 'new messages' icon was lit up. I flipped the silver lid.

The whole screen was taken up with one word. It was written over and over and over. *Nonononononononononononononon ononono*, all the way from the top of the little square to the bottom, in black letters on a swimming-pool-blue screen. I pressed the delete button but nothing happened.

I panicked. I threw the phone across the room and started to whimper. I looked at the silver phone on the floor and shook with fear. Who was sending me messages? There wasn't a signal in this room. I couldn't send any texts from here, so who was writing to me? And why were they saying 'no' over and over again?

I went to pick up the phone. *Don't be a fool*, I told myself. *It's just a phone. You can turn the stupid thing off, can't you?* I picked it up, half expecting it to be hot or something. The message was still there.

Then a thought occurred to me.

Sometimes, with long messages, you don't get the whole thing on the screen. You have to scroll down and the words go on. I clicked the side of the screen and the *nonononono* just kept on going, as if it would never stop. Then I saw it, right at the bottom, in the right-hand corner. It was a capital L. The rest of the text wasn't in capitals. I was ice cold all over. L was for Lily.

I pressed the 'delete message' buttons over and over again. The message vanished in the end. I got back into bed and hid my face in the pillow. I didn't want to see anything. I didn't want to hear anything. Amy would wake up and come in soon and I was still tired. I felt as though I'd had no sleep at all. And I was scared, really, really scared for the first time. Before now, I'd been puzzled, or a bit spooked, but I'd never felt like this before.

It crossed my mind that I didn't have to stay at Bowdon House. I could leave. I could tell Dr Slade that I wanted to go, or I could even run away. I could just pack my case and walk down the drive. He'd be upset, but he'd understand. Or even if he didn't, he couldn't stop me.

But if I did go, what would he think of me? He would think that I couldn't cope, that I hadn't got over my miscarriage. This was the proof, the fact that I was seeing ghosts. If I ran away, it meant that I was useless, whatever he might say. He wouldn't help me get another job, later on. I would have failed.

None of this matters, I told myself. *If it really gets bad, I can go. It's not that bad, is it?* I shivered but had to admit that it wasn't that bad. I could cope with it. What if there was the odd strange message on my phone and Amy was being tucked in by her dead mother? No problem. It was all in a day's work.

I must have fallen asleep. The next thing I knew was that Amy was sitting on top of me.

'Wake up, Marie. It's day. Poppy's here.'

I pushed down the duvet and made a face at her. 'I can't get up, not with you on top of me.'

She got off at once and took Poppy over to the dressing-table. 'Poppy thinks she's pretty. She is, isn't she?'

'She's the prettiest pig in the world,' I said. I got up and took my dressing-gown off the back of the door. 'You stay with her while I go and shower.'

When I came back, Poppy was lying on the bed.

'Has she finished looking in the mirror?' I said.

Amy frowned. She said, 'Mummy threw her on the bed. Poppy's sad. Mummy doesn't like Poppy.'

I tried to sound normal, although I felt a little sick. I said, 'I like her, though. And you like her, don't you, Amy? You told me last night you loved her.'

She nodded. She looked over her shoulder and then leaned towards me and whispered, 'I don't want Mummy to hear. I *do* love her, and you. I love you, Marie.'

I hugged her. I had tears in my eyes. I couldn't help it. I wanted to cry. Amy was the only person in the world, apart from Gran, who had ever said that to me. Rory never had. My mum never had or, if she had, I was too young to hear it. She'd stopped loving me by the time I understood what she was saying.

'And I love you, Amy,' I said.

I could feel her little body, right up against mine. I could hear her heart beating. I wouldn't have minded staying like that for ages, but she had other ideas.

'Let's take Poppy down to breakfast.'

'Okay. Wait while I dress and then we'll go and get you into some clothes.'

We had fun with Poppy Pig. Amy held her all day long. She came with us into the Wendy house. She drank lots of tea from little cups. She met Amy's dolls. When bedtime came, Amy chose Poppy Pig to sit on her pillow.

'Are you sure?' I asked. 'Won't Mr Snuggly mind not being in the bed?'

Amy shook her head.

I said, 'Okay, then, Poppy it is. Are you ready to say goodnight, Poppy?'

Amy held Poppy up and said, 'Oink, oink . . . That's yes.'

'Right. How about you? Are you ready?'

'Mmm,' she said, snuggling down under the duvet. 'You tuck me in, Marie.'

I didn't know what to do, what to say. Was Amy finally getting over the death of her mum? I thought, *She loves me. She said so. Tonight, she loves me as much as she loves Lily.* I felt happy about that. I felt proud that she'd chosen me to tuck her in.

'Okay,' I said. 'Here you go.' I pushed the duvet in around her body. I kissed the top of her head and said, 'Goodnight. Sleep tight.'

'Don't let the bugs bite,' she answered.

I stepped out into the corridor. The door of the little room next to the nursery stood open. I went to close it and I was sucked in. I know it sounds mad. Maybe people wouldn't believe me, but that's what happened. As soon as my hand touched the doorknob, I was pulled into the gloomy space and something, some force, slammed my body against the wall. The door clicked shut behind me and I was in the dark.

I cried out. I wanted to scream, but what came out was a kind of gasping sob. I lay down on the bed, and said, 'Let me out. Please let me out. Please. Please.'

It was freezing cold in there. I lay on the bed with my face pressed into the mattress because I didn't want to see what was in the room with me. Someone was, or something. I could hear breathing. Later on, I wondered whether what I'd heard was my own breath, but it wasn't that. I could hear the sounds I was making. I was sobbing and shouting out from time to time. This other noise was just *there* in the air around me.

Then everything went black.

11

'Marie? Are you okay?'

I opened my eyes and looked up. Kaye was standing in the doorway of the little room. She frowned at me. I must have looked strange.

She said, 'Is anything wrong? You look most odd.'

I got off the bed. What could I say? 'I felt a bit weird. I heard something in this room and then . . . I suppose I must have fainted.'

'You were making very odd noises. Come downstairs. I'll get you a drink or something. You're very pale. Or would you rather go and lie down? I could get Mrs James to bring you a tray with your supper on it. That's a horrid little room. I think it was used by Amy's mother when Amy was a tiny baby, when she had to get up in the night to feed her. Do you know what I mean? Now it needs redecorating. I haven't got round to it yet. Are you sure you're okay?'

'Yes, I'm fine. Thank you.'

I didn't want to be on my own. I wanted chatter and light and noise. I followed Kaye downstairs.

'Is Amy asleep?' she said. She was pouring me a glass of wine. 'Here, drink this. I know you're underage to drink, but not by much, right? You look as if you need it.'

'Thanks.' I sat down at the kitchen table.

'Here, do you fancy helping me with supper? I'm a bit useless but I said I'd do it. Can you chop a few vegetables?'

'Yes, I'm good at that.'

It was restful, sitting there, with Kaye chatting about nothing very much. What had happened in the little room faded away. I didn't forget about it. I just pushed it into a faraway place in my head. I tried to think about other things.

That worked fine until I went up

to bed. I'd left my phone on the bedside table. As soon as I came into the room, it started to ring. I froze just inside the door. *That's mad*, I thought. *There's no signal in this room.* I opened the phone. The screen was swimming-pool blue. I was shaking so much that the mobile nearly fell out of my hand.

I said, 'Hello? Gran, is that you?' I couldn't think of anyone else that it might be.

The noise that I heard wasn't words. It was just noise. It was like breathing with a sort of howl mixed into it. The howling came and went. At first, when I started listening, it was far away, but then it came closer. I threw the phone across the room in terror, but I couldn't leave it on the floor. I thought, *I'll press the 'call ended' buttons and that'll make it stop.* I picked up the phone with my arm stretched out as far away from me as it would go. I pressed the red button. The screen went black. I let out a breath that I didn't even know I'd been holding. Whoever had been on the other end had gone.

I put the phone down on the bedside table again and it rang just once. This meant a new text message.

I opened the phone and this time the message was *Gogogogogogogog ogogogo,* all the way down to the end of the screen. I knew there would be an L at the bottom.

I felt breathless and sick. What should I do? I had to do something. I didn't dare tell Dr Slade in case he sent me away. He wouldn't believe me. He'd think I was the crazy one. Doctors don't believe in ghosts. I had to rely on myself. What would happen, I wondered, if I sent a text of my own? Where would I send it?

I thought about this for a moment but I couldn't see a way to do it. Amy's phone used to belong to her mum, but that wasn't charged up. In any case, I didn't have the number.

Stop it, I told myself. *What are you doing, getting ready to send a text message to a ghost? You* are *mad. You must be.*

Mad or not, it made me feel better. I punched in a long text message. It said, 'Lily, I know it's you. Please stop. Amy is fine. I am fine. I love her. Go away. You are dead, Lily. I'm sorry to say that but it's true. You are dead now. Marie.'

Perhaps I was dreaming. Perhaps everything—the phone message, the text message, the whole thing—wasn't even real. I pinched myself. It was real.

I might as well send the message, but where to? I pressed the letters L-I-L-Y. Then I pressed the 'send' button.

I expected the screen to say 'message not sent' but it didn't. The little blue envelope that went sailing through the air showed that my text had gone somewhere, but not to Lily. How could it have done? It was bad enough to believe in ghosts without believing that they could get text messages. Someone, somewhere, would get a very odd text. I'd often got texts that weren't meant for me. I didn't care if it made someone feel a bit spooked to be told they were dead. It made *me* feel better. That was the main thing.

I wasn't scared any longer, but I kept my bedside lamp on until morning.

*   *   *

Lily came to me in a dream that night. At first, I wasn't afraid. I was having a normal chat with her. We were in the Wendy house. Amy was there, too, but not in the house. I could hear her playing outside the door. Lily was pouring tea into dolls' cups. She gave me a cup and said, 'Drink up.'

I sipped at it.

She said, 'Amy doesn't really like

you, you know. She's pretending. She loves me. Do you know that? Only me.'

'And her dad,' I said. 'She loves her dad too.'

Lily, the dream Lily, laughed. 'She doesn't see him much, does she?'

I didn't like the sound of her voice. It was just as if she was speaking under water. I could hardly hear her even though she was right next to me.

In the end, she vanished. Things are funny in dreams. She'd gone and was still there at the same time. I stopped being able to see her, but I felt her. She put an icy hand on my shoulder. My whole body froze. I couldn't move. Her voice was in my ear.

'You'll be gone soon. I'll always be with Amy. I'll never leave her. Never.'

*   *   *

In the morning, the dream was still in my head. Often, dreams go away when you open your eyes. You forget all about them. This one kept coming back to me all day. I was still hearing Lily in my head.

I played with Amy as usual. She took her mobile out of the pink bag at one point and began to listen. Then she put the phone back and zipped up the bag.

'Mummy says go away,' she said. She looked at the phone. 'Why did she say that?'

'I don't know, pet,' I said. 'Let's go and see what's for tea.'

Amy was sad all evening. 'I don't want you to go away, Marie. I love you. You can tuck me in, can't you?'

'Yes, of course I can. And I will,' I said. 'Don't worry.'

I wish now I hadn't said that. I shouldn't have tucked her in, ever. If I hadn't, maybe things wouldn't have turned out the way they did.

12

Next day, at bedtime, the really bad thing happened.

I was nearly ready to go up and tuck Amy in. She had had her bath. Mrs James had read her a story and gone up to her own room. I was in the kitchen getting her apple slices ready. Amy liked to eat them sitting up in bed, just before she brushed her teeth. I was on my way upstairs when the screams came.

I dropped the plate and ran up, taking two stairs at a time. I suppose the apple bits must have gone flying. I didn't care.

'Amy? Amy, what's wrong?' I shouted.

I rushed towards Amy's bedroom . . . The duvet looked as if a giant cat had been clawing it. It was ripped to pieces. The bottom sheet on Amy's bed was torn, too. Poppy Pig was on the pillow. Her tummy had been torn open and her stuffing was hanging out. She had no face. There was a piece of pink velvet on the floor by the bed. I could see one of Poppy's eyes on it. I nearly vomited. This was horrible. It was the worst thing I'd ever seen. Amy had vanished. There was no sign of her.

'Amy! Where are you?' I yelled.

She came out from behind the curtain. She'd been crying. I cuddled her to me.

'Sweetie, what happened? Tell me what happened.'

She shook her head. She wouldn't say a word.

I hugged her tight. 'Please, Amy, tell me what happened.'

She whispered in my ear, 'I mustn't tell. Mummy says I mustn't tell. Don't tell.'

Then Dr Slade and Kaye came rushing in. 'Amy!' he said and pulled her out of my arms. She began to wail. Kaye went over to the bed. She picked up the duvet and the torn sheet and took them away. She went downstairs and didn't come back.

Dr Slade said, over Amy's head, 'I'll deal with this now, Marie. I'll speak to you later.'

What was I meant to do? I went to my bedroom. I've never been so scared in my whole life. I picked up my mobile. The screen was black.

'Lily!' I shouted at the phone. 'Talk to me, please. Why have you done this to your own child? It's foul. *You're* foul. You're jealous of me. That's what it is, isn't it? Amy loves me. She loves *me*. GO AWAY! You're dead. YOU ARE DEAD!'

I couldn't help it. I burst into tears and went on crying. I don't know how long I cried.

By the time I came out of my room, Amy was asleep in the spare room. Her dad must have given her a pill to make her sleep.

I went downstairs to the kitchen. Dr Slade came in and asked me to go with him to his study. I followed him there. He told me to sit down. Then he looked at me. He spoke slowly. He was very calm, but I could tell that he was angry with me. I didn't know why.

'You know what I'm going to say, don't you?' he said. 'You'll have to leave Bowdon House, Marie, I'm sorry this has happened. I see now that I was wrong to ask a patient to work for me, even though you'd stopped coming to see me. Kaye will take you in the car tomorrow morning.'

'Why?' I asked. 'I haven't done anything wrong.'

He smiled. 'Well, that's a matter of opinion.'

I understood then. He thought I was the one who had cut up the duvet. He thought I was the one who had torn the sheet. He really *did* think Poppy Pig being torn to pieces was my doing. I didn't know what I could say to change his mind.

'I didn't do it, Dr Slade. I didn't do anything. I was downstairs when it happened. I'd never hurt Poppy Pig. I bought her for Amy. I'm telling the truth. You must see that.'

'If you didn't do it, who did?'

'You'll think I'm mad if I tell you.'

'No, I won't,' he said.

'It was Lily. She's jealous of me. Amy loves me. She even lets me tuck her in now. Did you know that?'

He smiled again. I know that kind of smile. He *did* think I was crazy, I could tell. He thought I was lying.

He said, 'I'll tell your gran you're ill, which you are, in a way. I think you ought to see a doctor, a specialist. It can't be me this time, I'm afraid. I can't help you now, because you've worked in my house. I'm so sorry, Marie, really. You're a good girl, but you must see, I can't have Amy exposed to such . . . well, to what I saw up there. Also, I should say this. You *could* have done what you did without knowing it. That kind of thing happens, you know. People forget what they've done or bury it in the back of their mind. Think about it.'

'NO!' I shouted at him then. 'I was downstairs. I was in the kitchen. I'd just cut up Amy's apples. I ran upstairs.'

'You could,' he said, 'have done the damage much earlier.'

'But I DIDN'T! I didn't. I never would—'

He spoke to me gently, as if I were sick. 'It couldn't have been Lily. She can't *do anything*, Marie. She's dead. She's buried. It *was* you, wasn't it? You'll feel better if you tell me.'

'Why would I do such a thing? I love Amy. You know I love her.'

He sighed. 'It's *because* you love Amy. You'd like her to be yours. It's *you* who are jealous. You're jealous of Lily. Amy plays games about her mother. She pretends to talk to her on the phone. You told me so yourself. You can't bear it. Don't

111

forget your own history, Marie. You'd like Amy to be your own baby. Have you seen Zoe lately?'

I shook my head.

'There you are then,' Dr Slade said. 'That proves it. My Amy has taken the place of your Zoe. I can't allow that, I'm afraid. I'm so sorry. You'll have to leave tomorrow. Go and pack now, please.'

*   *   *

They didn't let me see Amy again. I don't know where they took her. I didn't sleep well. I was crying most of the night.

When I got up in the morning, the house was silent. Mrs James was in the kitchen when I went downstairs.

'Where's Amy?' I asked.

'She has gone away with her father,' Mrs James said. She had her back to me. She wasn't going to tell me any more.

Kaye came in while I was drinking

my coffee. She didn't smile at me.

'Are you ready, Marie?' she said. 'Have you eaten?'

'I'm not hungry.'

'Right, then. We can go now if you like. Let's put your things in the car.'

'Goodbye,' I said to Mrs James. 'Thank you for everything.'

She turned to me then. I think she'd been crying too. 'Goodbye, dear. Good luck.'

I thought she was going to say something more, but she didn't. She sighed and then she turned away again. I think she felt bad about how things had ended for me. I hope she did. She couldn't say anything. She had to be loyal to Dr Slade, but even so I knew she liked me. I hoped she'd miss me a bit. She'd miss me coming to her room to watch TV. That's what I told myself. Maybe I was just making myself feel better.

I don't know why I thought Kaye was going to drive me all the way to Eastbourne but she didn't. She let me out at the end of the drive instead. She gave me an envelope with my wages in it. Then she said, 'The bus is due in ten minutes, Marie. Goodbye.' And that was that. She drove away fast.

*   *   *

When I was on the bus I took out my mobile. The signal was fine. I rang Gran.

'Gran, it's me. I'm coming home.'

'Why? What's wrong?'

'I've been sacked.'

'No, that can't be right. What for?'

'It's not—I can't say on the phone. I'll tell you later. Oh, Gran, I miss her. I miss Amy!'

'Don't fret, pet.'

I kept on crying.

Gran said, 'Didn't you hear? I said, *don't fret, pet*. You're meant to laugh. You always do when I say that. Remember?'

'I'm too sad, Gran. I can't.'

'Never mind, duck. You come home. I'll look after you. We'll be okay. Don't worry, really.'

'Okay. I'll try.'

I stared out of the window but I didn't see anything. One thought went round and round in my head. *What will they tell Amy? Where will they say I've gone?* It made me feel awful to think of her. What if they said I'd gone because I didn't love her any more? Would she believe that? I'd send her a card. I'd tell her the truth. I'd write, *I love you, Amy.* That made me feel a bit better.

Then I knew I couldn't do that. Dr Slade would tear up the card before Amy saw it. He wouldn't let me near her. He was scared of me. Well, you'd be scared, wouldn't you, if a mad person was writing to your kid?

Someone was sending me a text. I opened up the phone. 'One new message,' I read. There was a jumble of letters. The whole screen was full of total rubbish. *Dntsdoacny fivgaebaa ryghbgdabewtr fgbbvgawiebtasgov Sibdrasrtg oaadSbdrasrgds bairgb ocvA Lekt orfvn aOewhrt wsorhg Werj AVEIORGJ VZdknfs rnbvzav etuvwth s d a p o e w u t r o i h a p w e o r t v m t i o h g j a W o r v h t s t i f d s vrhbnflfqpirjgavwktev.*

I screamed and snapped the phone shut. Lily. It must have been Lily. No one else would send a message like that. She was laughing at me, saying, *I've won*. That's what the text meant. I knew it was what she felt. Amy belonged to her now, for ever.

I was shaking. The driver looked at me in his mirror and frowned at me. The window by my seat was open at the top. If I stood up, I could reach the opening. I took my mobile and threw it out as hard as I could. It flew out of the window. When I sat down again, a man sitting near me moved to the back of the bus. I couldn't blame him. I don't like to sit next to mad people on the bus.

13

Gran bought me a new phone. She wants me to go to another doctor. I don't know whether I want to speak to anyone. What would I say?

I'm trying not to think about Amy, but it's hard not to. Does she ever talk about me? I hope she does. I hope she still loves me. I'm sure she knows it wasn't me who tore up Poppy Pig. I'd never do a thing like that. Amy knows me. She knows I wouldn't do that. She just knows.

I was thinking about Amy when the phone rang. Gran was out at work, so I answered.

'May I speak to Marie?'

'This is Marie. Who's that?'

'It's Freda James. From Bowdon House.'

I nearly dropped the phone. I took a deep breath and said, 'Hello.' I couldn't think what else to say.

Mrs James said, 'Are you well, Marie?'

'Fine, thanks,' I said. 'How are you? And how's Amy?'

'Well, that's what I wanted to talk to you about.'

'How did you get my number?' I asked.

There was silence for a bit. Then she said, 'I looked in your file. It's in the study. That's where Dr Slade keeps his files. I'm not supposed to look at them, but I did—'

'Is anything wrong?'

'No, not really. It's just . . . Well, there's something I want to say to you.'

I could feel my heart thumping really hard. What could she possibly want?

She said, 'There's been . . . Something has happened.'

'What? What has happened?'

'I found Ruby in the Wendy house. Ruby is Amy's baby doll, do you remember? All her clothes were ripped and torn off her. And her hands and feet . . . Well, she had no hands and feet. It made me sick to see it, Marie. It did really. I think Amy must have done it herself. She was upset when you left. Perhaps this is her way of showing it.'

I closed my eyes. My poor little Amy. I didn't want to imagine what Ruby looked like.

'What did you do?' I said.

'I picked up the doll and put her in a carrier bag and threw her away in the bin. I've told Amy that Ruby has been lost and that we'll buy her another baby doll. It's her birthday on the 15th.'

'I don't know what to say, Mrs James. I wish—'

'You don't need to say a word. I had to tell you, that's all.'

I wanted to put the phone down. If I told Mrs James that Lily had broken off Ruby's hands and feet, she would not believe me. I nearly did but instead I said, 'Well, thanks for ringing. I'm glad you told me. Goodbye.'

'Marie? Are you still there?'

'Yes,' I said. 'I'm still here.'

'Amy often talks about you, you know. She really loved you. I could see that.'

'Thanks,' I said. 'Thanks for telling me that. Goodbye.'

I put the phone down then. It was kind of Mrs James to phone and it was nice of her to tell me that Amy still talks about me. And her birthday's on the 15th. I thought, *I could send her a birthday card. Lily can't object to that.*

I hope she doesn't. I'll send Amy a card. I remember the address. I know it off by heart.